MORRIS MacMILLIPEDE

The Toast of
Brussels Sprout

RED FOX READ ALONE

It takes a special book to be a
RED FOX READ ALONE!

If you enjoy this book, why not
choose another READ ALONE
from the list?

- **The Seven Treasure Hunts**
  Betsy Byars, illustrated by Jennifer Barrrett

- **Henry's Most Unusual Birthday**
  Elizabeth Hawkins, illustrated by David McKee

- **Cat's Witch and the Monster**
  Kara May, illustrated by Doffy Weir

- **Wilfred's Wolf**
  Jenny Nimmo, illustrated by Woody

- **Jake's Book**
  Kate Petty, illustrated by Sami Sweeten

- **Space Dog and Roy**
  Natalie Standiford, illustrated by Tony Ross

- **The Salt and Pepper Boys**
  Jean Wills, illustrated by Susan Varley

MICK FITZMAURICE

MORRIS MacMILLIPEDE

The Toast of
Brussels Sprout

ILLUSTRATED by SATASHI KITAMURA

RED FOX

A Red Fox Book

Published by Random House Children's Books
20 Vauxhall Bridge Road, London SW1V 2SA

A division of Random House UK Ltd
London Melbourne Sydney Auckland
Johannesburg and agencies throughout the world

3 5 7 9 10 8 6 4 2

First published by Andersen Press Limited 1994

Red Fox edition 1996
This Red Fox edition 1999

Printed and bound in Great Britain by
The Guernsey Press Co. Ltd, Guernsey, Channel Islands

RANDOM HOUSE UK Limited Reg. No. 954009

ISBN 0 09 940072 3

The Toast of
Brussels Sprout

1

Morris Macmillipede is eight years old and has 42 pairs of legs. And 42 pairs of feet. And 42 pairs of trainers.

His mother, Millicent Macmillipede, reads the Nine O'Clock News on Bee Bee Bee Television. His father, Mackintosh M. Macmillipede, is a policeman. He arrested the Ghastly Greenfly Gang and the Big Bad Bed Bug Brothers. Thanks to Mackintosh M., they're safely locked up in Woodworm Scrubs prison.

The Macmillipedes live at 26, Rhubarb Road in Brussels Sprout, the biggest insect city in Bell Lane Market. They have a four-bedroomed house made entirely of cabbage leaves. The problem is, they love the taste of cabbage, and they're forever nibbling at the walls and floors and ceilings. Mackintosh M. is always patching up holes to stop the rain coming in.

2

Brussels Sprout is a wonderful place for a young millipede. There are playgrounds with celery slides and radish roundabouts, and lovely, smelly gutters everywhere. On Saturdays, everyone goes to watch Earwig Rovers, the champions of the Football League.

But you'll never find Morris at the football match or playing with the other boys. For Morris has a secret.

It all started when he went with his school to see the Royal Insect Ballet. His friends were bored, but Morris

loved the theatre and the dancing and the costumes and the romantic music of Flykovsky. And most of all, he loved the ballerina, Dame Gossamer Spider.

'She's so beautiful,' he sighed, 'I wish I could share her web.'

Ever since that day, he's wanted to be a ballet dancer. He hasn't told his friends or his brothers, for he knows they'd laugh at him. But when the other boys go out to play, Morris stays at home and dances with his reflection in the mirror.

3

But Morris had to tell *someone* about his
dream or he'd explode. He decided to
tell his mother; surely she wouldn't
laugh? But Mrs Macmillipede *did*
laugh.

'A ballet dancer!' she said. 'Whatever
will you think of next?' She shook
Morris's head to make sure his brain
wasn't broken, then laughed all the
way downstairs to cook the dinner.

A tear rolled down Morris's cheek
and fell onto the carpet. His dream
would never come true; he'd never
dance with Dame Gossamer. If his own
mother laughed at him, who would take
him seriously?

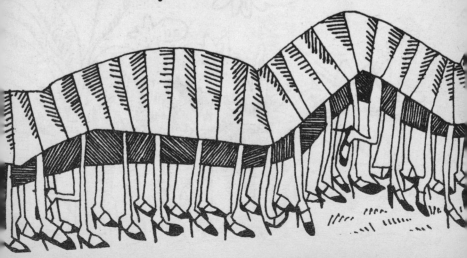

4

Morris crept out of his house and wandered sadly through the streets of Brussels Sprout. The afternoon slipped by and the sky grew dark. The Money Spiders went home from their offices, rushing to catch their trains.

'Stocks and shares,' they said to each other. 'Stocks and shares.'

Morris shivered as the icy wind sliced through his thin pullover. He was hungry, but all he had in his pocket was a piece of beetroot-flavoured bubblegum. He sat on a wall and chewed until the gum was soft and tasteless. Then he blew a broken-hearted little bubble.

Would his mother have missed him yet, he wondered? He felt so sad and lonely, he burst into tears.

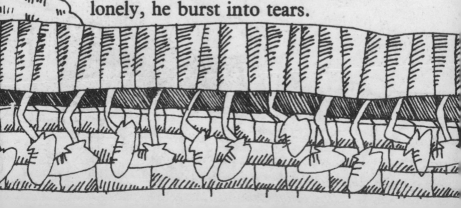

5

'Well!' said a gruff voice. 'You *do* seem sorry for yourself.'

Morris looked up. There stood an old Stag Beetle with a long, grey beard.

'If you were me,' sniffed Morris, 'you'd feel sorry too.'

'And why's that?' asked the old man, puffing at his pipe.

'Well . . .' Morris began, then told him all about his broken dream.

'Most unusual,' said the Stag Beetle when Morris had finished. 'Most boys want to play for Earwig Rovers or the England Crickets team. All the young

Beetles want to be pop stars. But you
want to be a ballet dancer.'

'Yes,' said Morris in a small voice,
hoping the old man wouldn't laugh.
And he didn't.

'If you want to do something badly
enough,' said the Beetle, 'you
shouldn't care what other people think.
And if at first you don't succeed, what
must you do?'

'Try and try and try again,' Morris
whispered.

'Quite right,' said the Beetle. Then
he puffed once more at his pipe and
shuffled away into the darkness.

6

By the time Morris arrived home, he was feeling much happier. He *wouldn't* care what people thought; he *would* try and try and try again.

He had a tasty tea of stale sprouts and squashed tomato, then lay on his bed thinking. Somehow he had to pay for ballet shoes and dancing lessons; but there was nothing in his money-box except a mouldy piece of chocolate.

What could he do? He stared sadly at his wallpaper with its rows of round, blue turnips. Then suddenly he had an idea. Round . . . paper . . . It was such a good idea that he set his alarm for five o'clock, nestled his 84 feet on his 84 hot-water bottles and fell fast asleep.

7

At five o'clock next morning, Morris
dragged himself out of bed. It was dark
and cold, and last night's wonderful
idea didn't seem so wonderful now.
But he wasn't going to give up.

He put on four pullovers and ran
along Rhubarb Road to Mr O'Wasp's
newsagent's shop. He'd seen the notice
in the window yesterday.

SMART BOY OR GIRL
WANTED FOR NEWSPAPER
ROUND

Morris pushed open the door. It was
lovely and warm inside.

'If it izzzzn't young Morrizzzz,'
buzzed Mr O'Wasp. 'And what can I
do for you?'

'I'd like a job,' said Morris.

8

He began work the next morning at half
past five. It was damp and misty, and
the bag of newspapers felt almost as
heavy as himself. But he didn't
complain; he just trudged round
Brussels Sprout delivering *The News
of the Worm* and *The Daily Snail*,
thinking about Dame Gossamer.

It all seemed worthwhile on Saturday
when Mr O'Wasp put ten pound coins
into his hand. 'Here are your
wagezzzzz,' he buzzed, and Morris ran
home and put the money in an old

biscuit tin under his bed.

In the months that followed, Morris often wanted to turn over and go back to sleep when his alarm clock went off. But he'd reach under the bed and feel the biscuit tin growing heavier and heavier, and he'd drag himself out into the cold streets once again.

On New Year's Eve, he decided it was time to count his savings. He tipped the coins onto his carpet . . . there was £120. It was enough! Tomorrow he'd go shopping!

9

Clutching the biscuit tin, Morris
pressed his nose against the shop
window. His eyes were wide with
excitement as he stared, not at toy
soldiers or train sets, but at a row of
dainty, pink ballet shoes.

He pushed open the heavy door and
went inside. Dark, wooden shelves
rose to the ceiling; faded photographs
of ballet dancers crowded the walls.
Everything in the shop seemed old, not
least the owner, a Great-Great-Grand-
Daddy Long Legs, who shuffled slowly
from the back room.

'Can I help you?' he wheezed,
looking at Morris over his gold-
rimmed spectacles.

'I'd like 42 pairs of ballet shoes,
please,' said Morris.

'That's enough for a whole school!'
exclaimed the old man.

'But they're all for me,' said Morris, pointing to his 84 feet.

The Great-Great-Grand-Daddy Long Legs counted out the shoes.

'There, young man. That'll be £84.'

Morris gave him the money, then ran home and went straight upstairs to his bedroom. It took ages to tie up all the laces, but finally he was ready. He looked at himself in the mirror and could hardly believe what he saw.

'Morris Macmillipede,' he whispered proudly, 'you're a real ballet dancer now.'

10

The Ballet School stood halfway along
Onion Avenue. Morris went nervously
inside and found a door marked

MADAME BUTTERFLY

He pushed open the door. Madame
Butterfly lay on a sofa dressed in
flowing silks of red and blue and yellow.

'I'd like to join your ballet class,' said
Morris timidly.

'Well!' she said. 'A millipede in a
ballet class! Whatever next!'

For a moment, Morris thought she
might be laughing at him; but she took
his money seriously and sent him off to
get changed.

11

When he pushed open the changing
room door, the other children stopped
talking and stared at him. Melanie
Mayfly tugged her pigtails.

'What are *you* doing here?' she
sneered. 'Millipedes can't dance.'

Everyone laughed, and Morris
wanted to run back home. But he bit
his lip and opened his eyes wide to stop
himself crying. Then he began to lace
up his shoes.

'What a slow-coach!' teased Melanie
Mayfly. 'The lesson will be finished
before he's even dressed.'

She stuck out her tongue at Morris

and fluttered across to the mirror.

'Oh, aren't I pretty?' she sighed.

By the time Morris had put on four pairs of shoes, the others were ready, and they ran out of the changing room leaving him quite alone. He heard music; the lesson was starting without him, and he had 38 pairs of laces still to tie.

He tried to hurry, but his fingers wouldn't go any faster; they just got caught up in the knots. It was nearly half an hour before he was ready and he tiptoed timidly into the hall to join the class.

12

The hall was high and wide, and all the walls were covered with mirrors. The children stood in lines facing Madame Butterfly, who sat at a very grand piano.

'You're late!' she snapped when Morris came in. But before he could explain about all the laces, she turned back to the class.

'Let me see you jump,' she said.

Morris stared in dismay as the children leapt gracefully into the air, hovered on their wings, then landed gently on the floor. He'd *never* be able to do that. But he remembered the old Stag Beetle's words and tried his best. He jumped with his back end; he jumped with his front end; he jumped with his middle. But he couldn't jump with all of himself at once. It seemed that millipedes simply weren't designed for jumping.

'You'll have to do better than that,' sighed Madame Butterfly.

But Morris couldn't do better. If only
he had wings! If only he didn't have
so many legs! It was a terrible start –
but worse was to follow.

'Now let me see your spins,' said
Madame Butterfly.

The children stood on one leg,
fluttered their wings and spun round
in perfect circles. It wasn't even worth
Morris trying.

He hung his head and crept out of
the hall. He'd never come back, and
his heart would never stop aching.

13

But that night, Morris dreamed of the old Stag Beetle and woke up feeling ashamed that he'd given up so easily. He *would* go back. He *would* try and try and try again. Let them laugh if they wanted to.

And he *did* go back. Oh, the other children giggled; Madame Butterfly sighed and snapped. But Morris took no notice. Each week he tried his hardest, and although he was still clumsy, he improved a little every time. And in the end, even Melanie Mayfly grew bored with laughing and left him alone.

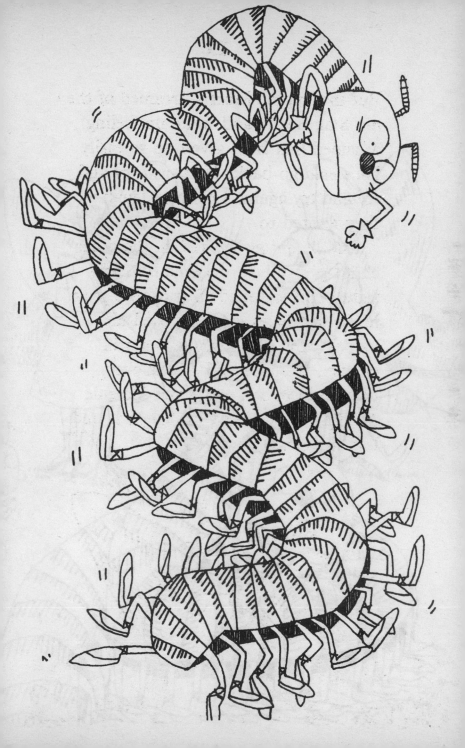

14

'Our Easter Concert is in four weeks' time,' said Madame Butterfly one day. 'We will be performing "The Sleeping Beauty". What a wonderful story! The Ugly Caterpillar sleeps in a cocoon for a hundred days, then turns into the Beautiful Butterfly.'

Melanie Mayfly was to be the Beautiful Butterfly, of course, and Martin Moth was to be the handsome Prince. Everyone else was given a part – everyone except Morris. As the others chattered excitedly, he coiled up sadly on his own in a corner. He'd tried so hard, but he wasn't good enough.

Madame Butterfly felt sorry for him. He was the worst pupil she'd ever had. But perhaps . . .

'Morris!' she called. 'Come here. I have a part for you. I want you to be the Ugly Caterpillar.'

15

Morris's part was small but very important. He had to spin across the stage into a huge silk cocoon; then Melanie Mayfly spun out of the other side as the Beautiful Butterfly. It was very difficult, and always made him dizzy. But he practised and practised until he could just about manage it.

Mrs Macmillipede made his Ugly Caterpillar costume, and all his family and friends bought tickets. As the concert drew near, Morris was so excited he couldn't concentrate at school. He was always in trouble with his teacher, Miss Louse.

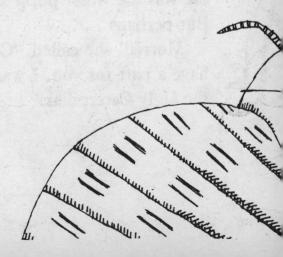

16

Finally, the great day arrived. The lights in the hall went down; the audience fell silent; Madame Butterfly played the first notes on the piano; then the curtain rose and Martin Moth began the ballet.

Half an hour later, they reached the great moment when Morris had to spin into the cocoon. Madame Butterfly played loud and fast, and Morris spun out onto the stage. Everything went perfectly, and as he approached the cocoon, he began to think of the applause he'd soon receive. But that was a terrible mistake, for he stopped thinking about spinning. His front end began to spin faster than his back end, and his long, clumsy body coiled up like a spring.

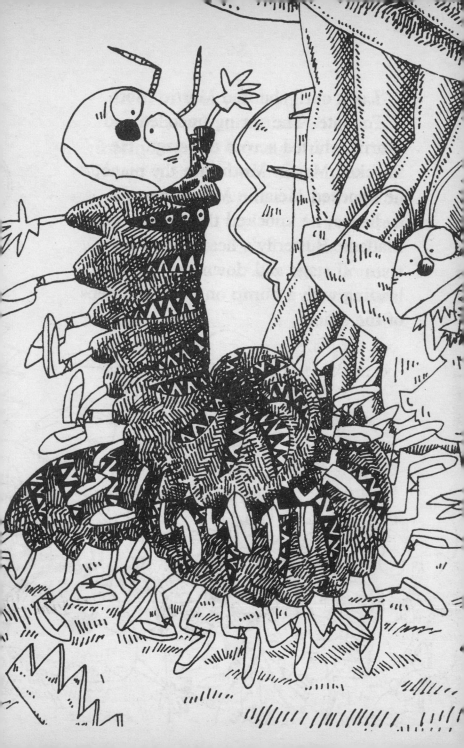

'Look out!' shouted Martin Moth.

Too late. The spring uncoiled and Morris whirled across the stage. He knocked Martin Moth into the piano; he knocked Melanie Mayfly into the audience; he knocked the scenery onto Madame Butterfly's head. Then he spun off stage and down the corridor, landing with a bump on the front steps of the school.

17

Morris had bruises everywhere, and his head wouldn't stop spinning. But the worst thing of all was the noise coming from inside – laughter. He'd made a fool of himself yet again.

He hurried away from the school and didn't stop until he reached the River Trickle. Leaning over Carrot Bridge, he stared down into the dark water. He was so miserable, he felt like throwing himself in. But he threw in his ballet shoes instead, all 42 pairs of them. They floated away into the night, taking Morris's dreams with them.

'Now, young man,' said a gruff voice. There was the old Stag Beetle, puffing away at his pipe. 'Tell me what happened.'

Morris told him the whole, sad story. 'So you see, I really did try and try and try again.'

'Indeed you did,' agreed the Beetle. 'But you see, my boy, millipedes just aren't made for ballet dancing. They have far too many legs.'

Morris felt cross; if that was the case, why had the old man encouraged him?

'But now I know you don't give up easily, I'll tell you what millipedes *are* made for,' said the Beetle.

Then he leaned over and whispered something in Morris's ear, so quietly you can't hear what he said. But it made Morris so happy, he clapped his hands and danced a jig round and round the old man.

18

Next evening, Morris went out after tea and came back two hours later with a great big grin on his face. When his mother asked him where he'd been, he just said, 'You'll see.' And he said the same thing every Thursday evening for the next six months.

One day, he came home and unrolled a bright yellow poster.

THE ORANGE CRATE THEATRE

PROUDLY PRESENTS MORRIS THE MIRACLE MacMILLIPEDE

SATURDAY SEPTEMBER 30TH 8.00PM

'What on earth are you up to?' asked his father.

'Just come and watch,' said Morris.

'The last time we came to watch you,' said his mother, 'you were the laughing stock of Brussels Sprout.'

But his parents agreed to come. And his brothers and all his friends bought tickets – they didn't want to miss Morris making a fool of himself again.

19

It was Saturday September 30th. The Macmillipedes drove to the theatre in their Ford Banana. What a crowd there was, all come to see Morris, all expecting to laugh at him.

At eight o'clock, the lights in the theatre went down, the curtain rose, and there in a spotlight stood Morris, wearing a top hat and tails. What would he do?

The conductor raised his arms, the orchestra set off at a tremendous pace, and Morris began to . . . TAP DANCE!

Tap tap tap went his left foot. T-t-t-t-t-tap went his right. T-t-t-t-t-t-t-tap. T-t-t-t-t-t-t-tap. T-t-t-t-t-t-t-t-t-t-t-t-t-t-t-tap. T-t-tap. T-t-tap. T-t-t-t-t-t-t-t-t-t-t-t-t-t-t-t-t-t-t-t-t-t-t-TAP.

The violinists' fingers flew; the pianist wished he had a hundred hands. But none of them could keep up with Morris the Miracle Macmillipede.

At the end of the show, the audience
clapped and cheered and threw
flowers. And best of all, not one person
in the whole theatre laughed.

20

There was a tremendous party in Morris's dressing-room that night; everyone wanted to be there to congratulate him.

'Well done!' said the old Stag Beetle. 'You really did try and try and try again.'

'I owe it all to you,' said Morris, giving the old man a hug.

'You owe it to all those legs of yours,' smiled the Beetle.

Morris's brothers and friends could hardly believe what had happened.

'We came to laugh,' they said. 'But we ended up cheering.'

Madame Butterfly kissed him on both cheeks.

'Darling!' she breathed. 'Didn't I always say you'd be a famous dancer one day?'

And Morris was feeling far too happy to remind her what she'd *really* said.

21

Next morning, the newspapers were
full of photographs of Morris, and the
phone didn't stop ringing all day. Every
theatre in the country wanted him to
appear. Each time he danced, he was a
huge success, and he was soon known
as Morris Macmillipede, the Toast of
Brussels Sprout. He was as rich as a
bluebottle, and he bought a house in
Celery Hills where all the famous stars
live.

Nothing could have made him any
happier. Or so he thought, until the
day the telephone rang.

'Hello,' said Morris.

'Oh, Mr Macmillipede, this is the
Orange Crate Theatre. Dame
Gossamer Spider is about to begin
rehearsals for a new ballet, which has
a most important part for a tap dancer.
We were wondering . . .'

RED FOX READ ALONES

THE SEVEN TREASURE HUNTS
Betsy Byars, illustrated by Jennifer Barrett

Jackson and his friend, Goat, like nothing better than hunting for secret treasure and trying to outwit each other. The fun only stops when Goat's big bad sister (known to them as 'the ogre') lays her hands on the special treasure Jackson has hidden. The treasure hunt to end all treasure hunts is about to begin . . .

ISBN 0 09 940112 6   £2.99

MORRIS MACMILLIPEDE
Mick Fitzmaurice, illustrated by Satoshi Kitamura

Morris MacMillipede's greatest dream is to be a ballet dancer, but his family just laugh at him. How can anyone with eighty-four feet possibly be a dancer? However, Morris plans to be the first millipede to partner Dame Gossamer Spider, the famous ballerina. Will his dream ever come true?

ISBN 0 09 940072 3   £2.99

HENRY'S MOST UNUSUAL BIRTHDAY
Elizabeth Hawkins, illustrated by David McKee

Aunt Jane and Aunt Charlotte always send Henry unusual birthday presents, but even he is surprised when he receives a tiny key and a zoo ticket. These two presents lead Henry to make some exciting new friends. Some are furry, some are four-legged, and some are BIG trouble!

ISBN 0 09 940132 0   £2.99

CAT'S WITCH AND THE MONSTER
Kara May, illustrated by Doffy Weir

Cat finds that his witch, Aggie, is not quite the witch he thought. There is a monster in the lake, and all the townspeople expect Aggie to get rid of it. She has even promised to do so – but there's just one little problem in the way. Can Cat help her qualify for the spell?

ISBN 0 09 940082 0   £2.99

WILFRED'S WOLF

Jenny Nimmo, illustrated by David Wynn Millward

Wolf leaves his snowy home for the warmer weather in England and, by great luck, finds his way to the kitchen of the poshest hotel in London: The Plush. The chef, Wilfred, loves wolves, and is all too happy to teach Wolf all his secrets. Just so long as the customers don't find out their cook is someone with shaggy fur and sharp teeth!

ISBN 0 09 940102 9 £2.99

JAKE'S BOOK

Kate Petty, illustrated by Sami Sweeten

Jake lives with his mum and dad and little sister Lily at 88 Albert Avenue – not forgetting Doris the cat and Mumpy the disappearing hamster. Here are lots of stories about the everyday, exciting things that happen to them all, from getting lost at the swimming baths to sledging in the snow.

ISBN 0 09 940122 3 £2.99

SPACE DOG AND ROY

Natalie Standiford, illustrated by Tony Ross

Roy Barnes has always wanted a dog, but the one which gets out of the spaceship that lands in his garden is rather more than he bargained for. What on earth can you do with a dog that hates dog food, reads newspapers and likes to use the telephone?

ISBN 0 09 940092 8 £2.99

THE SALT AND PEPPER BOYS

Jean Wills, illustrated by Susan Varley

Michael and his mother have come to the Seaview Ghost House (Ghost House?) for their holidays, where Lenny, the landlady's son, is a salt and pepper boy. He and Michael become firm friends, and a long summer of table-laying, tattoos, the dancing Floradoras and April and May, the dreaded 'kissing cousins', is right round the corner!

ISBN 0 09 940142 8 £2.99

Mrs Pepperpot stories by Alf Prøysen

Mrs Pepperpot, the little old lady with a BIG problem!
Any minute, she can find herself shrinking to the size of a tiny
pepperpot. And then all sorts of amazing adventures begin!

Little Old Mrs Pepperpot

How can Mrs Pepperpot visit her friends, get the supper
cooked and stop the cat from thinking she's a mouse? And
what will happen when she gets shut in the macaroni drawer?
ISBN 0 09 938050 1

Mrs Pepperpot Again

Minding the baby, catching mice and dealing with an
enormous moose are not all that easy when you're the
size of a pepperpot.
ISBN 0 09 931800 8

Mrs Pepperpot's Outing

A day out in the countryside turns into one adventure after
another for poor Mrs Pepperpot. Falling into an ice cream
mountain is no treat when you're tiny!
ISBN 0 09 957410 1

Mrs Pepperpot's Year

Mrs Pepperpot is kept busy all year round:
being adopted by a hen, saving her friend
the moose from being hunted and
cheering up a little girl in hospital.
ISBN 0 09 926727 6

"Timeless Scandinavian magic"

Stephanie Nettell
The Guardian

Out now in paperback
from Red Fox, priced £2.99

THE RUNTON
WEREWOLF
Ritchie Perry

*'I suppose I ought to mention one minor fact about myself -
I'm a werewolf. Yes, that's right, I'm a werewolf.
So is Dad, and my mum is a vampire...'*

By day Alan's a normal schoolboy. But at night his 'gronk factor' kicks in - and suddenly, he's not your average kind of guy...

THE RUNTON WEREWOLF
When a legendary werewolf is spotted running through Runton, Alan uncovers an amazing family secret - and suddenly his hair-raising bad dreams begin to make sense...

THE RUNTON WEREWOLF
AND THE BIG MATCH
Alan's just got to grips with being a Gronk (a nice, friendly werewolf) only to discover that a couple of mad scientists are hot on his trail. Poor Alan - it looks like it's all over...

THE RUNTON WEREWOLF by Ritchie Perry
Red Fox *paperback*, ISBN 0 09 930327 2   £2.99

THE RUNTON WEREWOLF
AND THE BIG MATCH by Ritchie Perry,
Red Fox *paperback*, ISBN 0 09 968901 4   £3.50

Bumwigs and Earbeetles

and other Unspeakable Delights

Poems by ANN ZIETY
Illustrated by LESLEY BISSEKER

Think ghastly! Think grisly! Think grim!
BUMWIGS AND EARBEETLES is all those
things... and worse!!!
Smelly socks, crumbly compost heaps and mangy
moggies are among the unthinkable, unspeakable
delights in this collection.

Catch a whiff of this...

MY DOG NEVER HAD FLEAS

he had bumwigs and earbeetles
and sinus larvae
and one or two exaggerated boils
and bits of ticks that stuck to his ears
and sticky mites
and bites from fights
and stashes and stashes of nasty rashes
but he never had fleas
not one

RED FOX paperback, £3.50 ISBN 0 09 953961 6